## FIRST FLIGHT®

*FIRST FLIGHT® is an exciting
new series of beginning readers.
The series presents titles which include songs,
poems, adventures, mysteries, and humour
by established authors and illustrators.
FIRST FLIGHT® makes the introduction to
reading fun and satisfying
for the young reader.*

*FIRST FLIGHT® is available in 4 levels
to correspond to reading development.*

### Level 1 – Pre-school - Grade 1
Large type, repetition of simple concepts that are perfect
for reading aloud, easy vocabulary and endearing
characters in short simple stories for the earliest reader.

### Level 2 – Grade 1 - Grade 3
Longer sentences, higher level of vocabulary, repetition,
and high-interest stories for the progressing reader.

### Level 3 – Grade 2 - Grade 4
Simple stories with more involved plots and a simple
chapter format for the newly independent reader.

### Level 4 – Grade 3 - up (First Flight Chapter Books)
More challenging level, minimal illustrations for the
independent reader.

**A First Flight® Level Three Reader**

# Andrew, Catch that cat!

By

Deanne Lee Bingham

Illustrated
by Kim LaFave

Fitzhenry & Whiteside • Toronto

FIRST FLIGHT® is a registered trademark of Fitzhenry and Whiteside

First published in the United States in 1999.

Fitzhenry & Whiteside acknowledges with thanks the support of the
Government of Canada through its Book Publishing Industry Development
Program in the publication of this title.

Printed in Hong Kong.

Design by Wycliffe Smith Design.

10 9 8 7 6 5 4 3 2 1

Canadian Cataloguing in Publication Data

Bingham, Deanne Lee, 1963-
Andrew — catch that cat

(A first flight level 3 reader)
ISBN 1-55041-411-9 (bound)
ISBN 1-55041-413-5 (pbk.)

1. Cats — Juvenile fiction.  I. LaFave, Kim.  II. Title.  III. Series.

PS8553.I64A75 1999      jC813'.54      C98-932939-9
PZ7.B511816An 1999

*With love, for my aunts—*
*Marilyn, Betty and Doris and my uncles—*
*Alec and Lloyd and in loving memory of my*
*Uncle Malcolm*

Deanne

*To Jeffery*

—K.L.

# AndreW, CAtCH tHAt CAt!

# Chapter One

Sarah hopped onto Andrew's bed.
"Good kitty," yawned Andrew.
He scratched behind her ear.
Sarah purred.

Andrew's bed was one of Sarah's
favorite places to curl up. She knew
all the best spots in the house.

After all, she was an indoor cat.

Andrew went downstairs
for breakfast.

"Look!" said his little brother,
Matthew, as he pointed outside.
"The robins are splashing in the
birdbath."

Sarah's tail quivered back and forth like a cobra. She meowed to go outside.

Andrew looked at Sarah and said "No kitty, you are an indoor cat."

## Chapter Two

After breakfast, Andrew opened
the door to the backyard, and went
to wait for his best friend, Josh.

Josh needed Andrew's help.
He wanted to earn some money
to buy his mother a birthday gift.

He tried to walk dogs,
but their leashes
got tangled.

He tried to sell
lemonade, but
his best
customers
were wasps.

He even tried
to have a craft
sale, but no one
wanted to buy
clay sculptures or
macaroni necklaces.

Andrew and Josh sat down to think.

Matthew sat down beside them.

"Who left the door open?"
called Andrew's dad.

Andrew's dad thought he saw
the white tip of a cat's tail.

He looked over the fence and
into the neighbor's backyard.

"Sarah's out! Andrew, catch that
cat!" he yelled.

# Chapter Three

Mr. Martin heard Andrew's dad. He ran to his backyard.

He didn't notice that his wife was smoothing the wet cement that would soon be a patio.

Andrew raced to the fence.
"On no!" he shouted in surprise.

But Andrew couldn't stay,
he needed to find Sarah.

Andrew ran toward the sidewalk.
Josh followed.

"I'll help," offered Josh.

"Find Sarah, Rex! Catch that
cat!" he told his dog.

Andrew and Josh
saw the white tip
of a tail around the
corner of Mr. Lee's house.

Rex raced ahead after the tail.

Mr. Lee's dog
raced after
Rex.

The two dogs began to play,
darting back and forth.

They rolled in the garden.

They wagged their tails and barked.

They chased each other around and
around Mr. Lee's prize rose bushes
until both dogs were dizzy.

Next door, Mr. and Mrs. Layton were busy weeding their garden.

"Have you seen Sarah?" Andrew asked.

"I thought I heard something under the porch," said Mr. Layton.

Mr. Layton bent down to look.

"It's way back there," he whispered.

He slowly crept under the porch.
Cobwebs stuck to his hair and face,
and old brown leaves crunched
beneath him.

Mr. Layton could see two eyes glowing in the dark. "Here, kitty," he said softly, as he reached out.

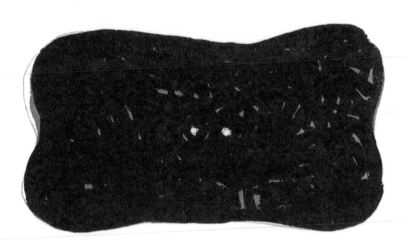

Just then, Mrs. Layton returned with a flashlight and shone it under the porch.

Andrew saw black fur like Sarah's.
Then he saw a long white stripe
down the animal's back.

It raised its tail. Mr. Layton howled.

"Run!" shrieked Mr. Layton,
and Andrew did.

# Chapter Four

Josh was still looking for Sarah
when he met up with Andrew.
They walked toward
Miss De Val's house.

Miss De Val was humming
as she carried a delicious
two-layer cake to her car.

From behind the parcels
piled on the sidewalk, Andrew
could see something twitching.
It looked like black ears.

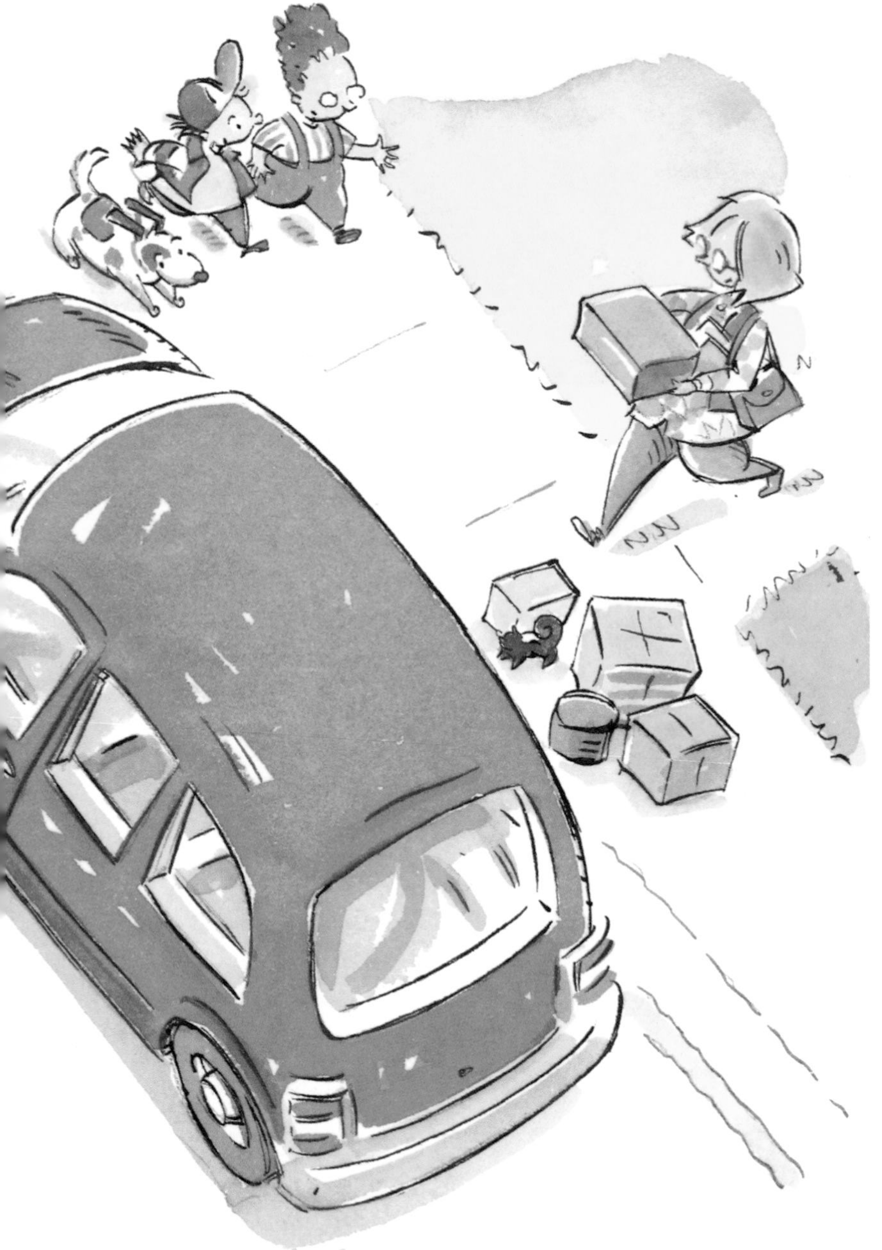

Rex saw them, too. He rushed
toward the parcels with
Josh close behind.

Rex ran between Miss De Val's feet.

Then Rex started running circles around Miss De Val.

Miss De Val struggled to untangle herself from his leash.

"Woof!" barked Rex.

Miss De Val was so startled
that she lost her balance
and tumbled to the ground.

Buttercream frosting and the
French vanilla cake burst out
of the box, and splattered in
every direction.

Frightened by the commotion,
a little black squirrel scampered
away.

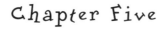

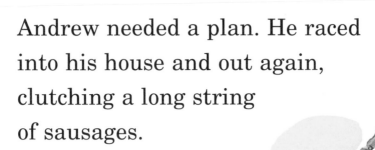

# Chapter Five

Andrew needed a plan. He raced
into his house and out again,
clutching a long string
of sausages.

They were Sarah's
favorite treat.

"Here, kitty, kitty, kitty,"
called Andrew.
Nothing happened.

Andrew waved the string of
sausages in the air. "Here, kitty,"
he called. Still nothing happened.

He swung them above his head.
Then he ran and jumped
and twisted until
every last sausage
had wound around him.

Finally, a cat appeared.
Then another cat and another cat.

But no Sarah.

The cats began purring
and rubbing against
Andrew's legs.

One cat lunged for
a sausage and missed.
"Yikes!" howled Andrew.

Still more cats came. Hungry,
noisy cats. Andrew was
outnumbered.

Andrew ran along the sidewalk.
The cats ran along
the sidewalk.

Andrew dashed through the
sprinkler puddles.

The cats dashed through the
sprinkler puddles.

Andrew jumped over
a bright red
wagon.

The cats
ran under, over,
and around the bright red wagon.

Then Rex came running up
to Andrew.

Rex caught the sausages
and raced down the street.

The cats
raced after him.

A woman was showing
a house to a new family.

She opened the door and in raced
Rex, followed by all the
neighborhood cats.

Then it started to rain.

## Chapter Six

Andrew went home. He sat at the window, watching the rain falling harder and harder against the glass.

He missed the way Sarah would curl around him and purr.

He missed the way Sarah would cuddle into his lap.

"Time to eat," said Andrew's mom.
"We'll look again after lunch."

Andrew joined his family at the
table. He tried to pull his chair out,
but it was stuck. He pulled again
and it still wouldn't budge.

He lifted the tablecloth and
something started to move.

A tail was twitching under the table.

"Oh, Sarah," Andrew groaned. "I've
been looking for you all morning."
Sarah stretched and yawned.

"Sarah was home all along,"
Dad sighed.

"Well, Dad," said Andrew,
"she *is* an indoor cat!"

# Chapter Seven

That night, after all the excitement, Andrew had an idea. He and Josh could earn money by helping repair all of the damage.

The next morning Andrew and Josh made dozens of flyers.

Then they filled the wagon with brooms, rakes, buckets, and rags, and went door to door.

Their flyers read:

Two Boys
& a Wagon
· We tidy yards
· wash cars
· trim brushes
· plant flowers
· walk dogs
· clean under porches
(without skunks)

By the end of the week, Josh had enough money to buy his mother a wonderful birthday gift.

Andrew used his earnings to buy a favorite treat for a special friend.

## Other Books in the
## First Flight® series